Setting the scene

Marcus is getting ready to start his new apprenticeship, but when he gets the details of the company he will be working for,

he's confused. Sunflower and Co – what's that? Turning up at his first day on the job, Marcus isn't hopeful – until he discovers that Sunflower and Co is actually a crime investigation agency. His boss is the formidable Mrs Sunflower, who turns out to be quite an unusual boss – and Marcus has plenty more magical surprises coming his way.

Reading investigation

Can Marcus help Sunflower and Co save London from the werebats?

Chapter 1

Never be the last to put your name down on the list.

That lesson came too late to save Marcus Sealford. His life was officially over – and all because he'd had to take his little sister to nursery. No one else could do it. His mum had twisted her ankle, Gran was in hospital and their neighbour was on holiday. It had to be him. He had known as soon as he had walked into City Academy an hour late on Apprenticeship Day that he had lost out.

"Hey, mate, what's Sunflower and Co?" asked Callum, pointing at Marcus's name on the printout.

"No idea. You got Pinewood Studios?" asked Marcus.

Callum tried not to look too pleased, though his spiked

brown hair seemed to be leaping up with extra joy this morning. He knew that Marcus had desperately wanted the training scheme at the film studios, but the careers adviser, Ms Faye, told Marcus that his application had been submitted too late. Marcus was sure it hadn't been, but she'd insisted.

"I bet it's only making coffee or sweeping up," said Callum, trying to keep a straight face.

"Yeah, but making coffee or sweeping up on the set for *Star Wars*, or *James Bond*," said Marcus, grumpily.

Callum grinned. He couldn't help himself. "I know. How great is that?"

"You don't even know anything about film," said Marcus. Film was Marcus's hobby. He was the one who watched all the YouTube videos for young filmmakers, who listened to the podcasts and who went to the cinemas as often as he could afford it. Callum couldn't name a single film director.

"I'll learn, won't I?" said Callum. "Lighten up! Maybe at Sunflower, you'll learn stuff too?"

"Yeah, maybe."

Taking himself off to a quiet corner of the school, Marcus searched for his new employer online. The name sounded so lame. But there was nothing. No website. No social media. No details of a company of that name at the address that he'd been given.

He tried to imagine what it could be. A business that sold gardening stuff? But Shoreditch was in the middle of London. There weren't many gardens around that part, just lots of narrow streets, old buildings and council estates. A florist? Please, no. He could imagine exactly what fun Callum and his other mates would have if they found him arranging bouquets of roses and carnations for a living. But it had to be legit, didn't it, to be part of the government apprenticeship scheme?

"So, Marcus, you will be doing your apprenticeship with Sunflower and Co," said the careers adviser, Ms Faye. She was a tall woman with a twist of black hair that curled over her shoulder like a snake, and she seemed to be able to appear out of nowhere.

"Do I have to?"

"You signed up for the scheme. All seventeen-year-olds must be in education or a training scheme, you know that," replied Ms Faye.

Marcus did know that, but it didn't make it any better.

"Let me give you a word of advice. Don't be late. Mrs Sunflower is a troll about bad manners," said Ms Faye. She gave Marcus a strange smile and then glided off to talk with the other apprentices. She was soon congratulating Gina Haskins on her apprenticeship at a local patisserie.

Gina wanted to be a pastry chef and her ambition was to win the *Bake Off* TV show. Gina was joined by Callum and soon both of them were laughing with smug delight. All his old friends were sailing off to their shiny futures and he got what? A big yellow flower and a troll of a boss.

* * *

Marcus hopped off the bus and checked his phone against the map he'd been given. That was weird: there was no reception, not even a Wi-Fi network he could join. He'd have to do this old style. Turning the map, he held it the way he needed to walk.

The address was 'Goblin Alley', which sounded like something out of *Harry Potter* – but then he saw the sign on the brick wall. The arrow pointed between two empty shops. If he didn't have his map, he would think it was the back way to the bins, not a proper street. You could get a bike down there, but not a car.

It got darker as he went further down the alleyway. The smell was bad too, like sour milk. No respectable business would set up shop here, would it? Customers would be too afraid to come down this dark alley. This was exactly the kind of place a mugger could lurk because no one would see them strike their victim. Street smarts alerted, Marcus wondered if he should turn around and go back to school. He would tell Ms Faye that he couldn't find the place.

That was when he saw the sign blinking over the entrance to an abandoned warehouse. The windows were boarded up and the upper floor was smoke-damaged.

"You've got to be kidding," muttered Marcus.

It didn't say Sunflower and Co. It said 'YOU ARE IN THE RIGHT PLACE'. That would've been creepy enough, but the blinking part was his own name: 'MARCUS'.

What choice did he have but to go in? He had to hand it to them – they were good at making the apprentice feel welcome, even if he didn't want to be there.

He pushed the bar on the fire door and walked in.

It was like stepping into another world. Gone was the wrecked building – inside, it glowed softly, like the seashell his dad had got him from the Caribbean. Everything was a pearly white: walls, carpet, desks and chairs – everything apart from the computer screens, which were deep-space black, and the blue cat that sat on top of a filing cabinet.

It winked at Marcus with amber eyes.

Heavy footsteps approached Marcus from behind.

"You're late," said a gruff voice.

Marcus spun round and looked up. And up. And up.
Marcus was tall for his age, but this woman topped
him by a metre. She was broad too, like her natural
shape was that of an American football player in
their protective gear, though her chosen outfit was
a powerful black suit. His gaze landed on her face.
Marcus had never seen a woman with a snout, tusks
and red eyes.

She glared at him. "So? I'm a troll. Get over it."

"W... what?" Marcus pressed his fingers to his
forehead, wondering if he was dreaming.

"It's your first day, so just this once, I'll forgive you for being late." She held out a hand, her fingers thick and pointed like claws, with nails painted purple. "Welcome to Sunflower and Co," she growled.

Quiz

Literal comprehension

Page 5 – What does Marcus find out about his apprenticeship placement before he arrives on his first day?

Inferential comprehension

Pages 2–4 – Why is Marcus so disappointed with his apprenticeship placement?

Personal response

Page 9 – How would you feel if you found yourself in Marcus's position, standing in front of Mrs Sunflower?

Chapter 2

This had to be a dream, right?

"You look surprised," said Mrs Sunflower.

"You could say that," Marcus pinched himself to test that he was awake and it was all really happening. It was!

"I'm Mrs Sunflower. Welcome to London's premier Alternative Crime Investigation Agency, Sunflower and Co. You will be working with Tania. She was the one who wanted us to take on another apprentice, so she gets babysitting duty."

"Babysitting!" Marcus objected. "I'm not a baby!"

"I hope she takes better care of you than she did the last apprentice. Anything else you'd like to know before I go out? I have a dragon egg hunter to arrest before midday." She twisted her arm to look at the tiny gold watch strapped to her wrist.

"Er..." began Marcus.

"Good. I'll see you later." She clapped him on the shoulder, making his knees bend, and strode out.

When the door clanged behind her, Marcus looked around the empty warehouse. None of the desks were occupied though there were workstations for five employees. He went over to the blue cat and stroked it.

"Are you Tania?" he asked the cat.

"Don't be silly, that's Beckham." A tiny woman slid down a fireman's pole from the upper floor. Marcus blinked. For a second, it looked like she had wings, but then she became totally normal – just a girl in jeans and a t-shirt. Her hair was a fiery shade of red and she had a ruby stud in her nose. "I'm Tania Firebird."

"I'm... er... Marcus Sealford." He shook her hand, surprised to find she had a grip like barbed wire.

"Ouch."

"Sorry! I must remember to retract my claws. So, I'm your mentor for your apprenticeship. Welcome to real life. No more school lessons, no more detentions, no more canteen meals. With us, you will learn how to survive on the mean streets, how to arrest criminals with magical powers and never to eat food from fairyland. Got it?"

Marcus sat down in the chair which scooted back on its wheels.

"Let me guess – is this like some theatre school thing? Are you all actors?" asked Marcus.

Tania giggled. "I do so love it when a Normal tries to make sense of us." She tapped his nose. "Wake up, Marcus. Blink. Open your eyes. There is far more to the world than dreamt of in your philosophy."

"Hey, that's a quote from Shakespeare, isn't it? So, it *is* a theatre school!" Marcus felt pretty pleased having remembered that quote from his English class.

"Wrong, kiddo. Shakespeare stole that line from me. He was one of our first apprentices," explained Tania.

Marcus pretended he got the joke. "This is all a big act then? Well done to Mrs Sunflower for going to all the trouble of wearing the troll mask and fake tusks. Was she on stilts? Was that why she was so tall?"

Tania rolled her eyes. "You're going to be difficult to persuade, aren't you? You see a troll and think someone is in a costume. You catch sight of my wings and tell yourself you're dreaming. This is such a waste of my time." She jumped up. "Look carefully. Use your other sight."

"My other what...?" asked Marcus.

"Blink!"

He blinked. Yellow wings tipped with orange burst from her back and she hovered in the air.

"Whoa!" exclaimed Marcus, falling off his chair. She flew once round the filing cabinet then landed back where she began.

"I'm a firebird. Legendary magical creature from Eastern Europe. But don't you dare try to pluck one of my feathers. It would not go well for you."

Marcus held up his hands. "I won't," he promised. Could this day get any stranger?

"Excellent. Then we will get on okay," said Tania.

"So, is the cat, like, magic too?" asked Marcus.

"All cats are magic," said Tania, rolling her eyes at Marcus's ignorance. "I thought you'd know that much. Follow me." She headed to a room marked 'Danger'. Marcus eyed the 'Danger' sign with unease.

"What's in there?"

"Our supplies," said Tania.

"What, like, weapons and ammunition?" he asked.

Tania swung round on him, fire crackling from her fingertips. She stuck one pointy end in his chest. "Dude, we do not use weapons. Ever. You get me? Instant expulsion from Sunflower if you do that."

"So, no taser guns?" said Marcus.

"Nope."

"What do you use?"

"See for yourself." She stepped aside to reveal shelves upon shelves of crisps, chocolate and soft drinks. "Stock up. Working for Sunflower and Co involves lots of long hours watching the bad guys. Fuel is essential." She tucked some trail mix into her pocket.

"So why was the door marked 'Danger'?"
asked Marcus.

"Have you ever worried about what your teeth will be like when you are older?" She looked at him. "I guess not. You must be, what? Under a hundred?"

"I'm seventeen."

She clicked her fingers. "Right. I keep forgetting. You need to understand, when you are an immortal creature like most of us here, you have to look after your teeth. You don't want to spend an eternity with cavities, do you? And human snacks have got so good recently." She sighed and picked up a chocolate bar. "See? Fatal." She put it back.

Marcus didn't need to be asked twice. He picked up a selection of chocolate and two packets of crisps.

"Before we go," Tania looked at Marcus "you must agree to our code of conduct."

Marcus had decided a few minutes back, probably when he saw the free food, that just going along with this was the best way. He could worry about what was real and what was make-believe when he got home. Besides, he would have mega bragging rights when he saw Callum. At Pinewood, they only *made* movies, this was like being in one.

"Okay. Hit me with it," said Marcus.

"One: you will tell no one about us."

His dreams of bragging rights fizzled out like a sparkler.

"Two: you will not share details about your missions, not even with colleagues, unless cleared by Mrs Sunflower."

"Got it. No shooting my mouth off."

"Three: you will not use magic in front of a Normal unless your life is in danger."

That one was easy. He had no magic, not even a card trick. "Sure. Wait! Is my life likely to be in danger?" asked Marcus, anxiously.

"Not if things go to plan." She headed for the exit. "Not that they usually do go to plan. Are you coming?"

Quiz

Literal comprehension

Page 17 – Why are human snacks so dangerous, according to Tania Firebird?

Inferential comprehension

Page 11 – Mrs Sunflower says that she hopes Tania takes better care of Marcus 'than she did the last apprentice'. What does this suggest?

Prediction

Page 15 – Tania warns Marcus: '... don't you dare try to pluck one of my feathers. It would not go well for you.' What do you think might happen if Marcus plucks one of Tania's feathers?

Chapter 3

Should Marcus go with Tania? He knew that he could turn right and head back to school. He would get grief from Ms Faye for giving up on his apprenticeship, but he could survive that. Or go left and follow the firebird? That way lay life-threatening danger and a world he never knew existed.

He went left.

Tania walked him to the local park. So far, so familiar.

"Let me tell you what you need to know." She looked at him, her emerald eyes hot like a gas flame. "We were once one of the Others. From the Other Land."

"Ri-ight." said Marcus.

"Marcus Sealford, don't you roll your eyes at me!" she said. That wasn't fair, she didn't go five minutes without rolling hers at one of his comments.

"Alright, I won't," he said. "But this is a lot to take in."

"Hurry up and adjust. London sits on a crossroads between worlds," explained Tania.

"You're not talking worlds like Disneyland Paris or World of Sofas, I guess?" Marcus joked.

She sighed impatiently. "Have you ever wondered why London Bridge keeps falling down?"

"It hasn't, not since it was replaced a couple of centuries ago."

Tania snorted. "That's like yesterday to me. It fell down each time the Others invaded and collapsed the old structure in their warfare with Usworlders."

"Usworlders?" asked Marcus.

"Us exiles from the Other Land. We are refugees and call ourselves Us to separate ourselves from the Others who still live there. Have you ever wondered about the flock of ravens in the Tower of London – why do they have to remain there?"

"Is this a trick question? Isn't there some legend about disaster if the ravens leave?" asked Marcus. He'd been on the school trip to the Tower. He remembered the Beefeaters in old-fashioned red uniforms, grisly tales about beheadings and a flock of birds.

"The ravens protect the Crown Jewels," said Tania.

"Who is trying to steal them?" asked Marcus.

"The Otherworld gangs who want to add the Crown Jewels to their treasury."

"If you say so," said Marcus.

"Marcus, forget fairyland and pixie dust, the Otherworlders are tough guys who would trample the human gangs of London into the dust and dance on their bones. They've taken over the parallel world of the Other London and are now trying to take over ours. They only used to break into our territory, steal things, make trouble and then run back. Now they are staying and occupying parts of this world," explained Tania.

That sounded worrying. "What Other London?" asked Marcus.

"You didn't think this was the only one, did you?" She waved at the city all around them.

"Anyway, Us refugees, like Mrs Sunflower and myself, are doing our best to stop the Other gangs from coming here, but it is tough and we look like we're losing as more parts of our London turn Other."

This was doing his head in. "There are parts of London that have turned Other? Why has no one noticed?"

"Because they've all dropped off the maps and become no-go areas for humans. You won't be able to find them on your phone. Humans have been put under a spell to forget they existed."

"I suppose that's pretty bad?" asked Marcus.

"Very bad. And now you, Marcus, have been recruited to join the battle to stem the flood of Other crime in the capital."

They had arrived at the café kiosk and Tania joined the queue. Buying a roll, she headed for the pond and began to feed the ducks. Marcus set off to walk around the pond, trying to take in everything she had said. Part of him still believed it was all a bizarre joke and that the punchline would come soon, but most of him now believed her. He had to rethink things.

If any of this was true, then it was time to get serious. He returned to Tania, his hands in his pockets.

"So when do I get to find out about this mission I'm going on?"

"It's already started," replied Tania.

"Our mission is feeding ducks?" he said, in disbelief.

"No," said Tania, "your mission isn't feeding ducks. I want you to look around you and tell me what you see."

Marcus listed the things he could see. "Pond, ducks, parents with kids in pushchairs, playground, grass, trees."

"Look harder," insisted Tania.

"This is stupid." Marcus kicked the pond railing.

"No. The only thing that's stupid is not being prepared," said Tania.

"Okay, okay," said Marcus, as he pulled out a chocolate bar and snapped open the wrapper.

Tania threw the last bits of roll to the ducks. "Come on, Marcus, you must see it now." She stared at the crumbs being gobbled up by the boldest duck. "Maybe we were wrong about you? Maybe you aren't one of us?"

Marcus thought hard. He was determined to prove that he could do it. He remembered how he had been able to see Tania as a firebird when he blinked. He tried that now and blinked three times. On the third blink, something flickered in the trees at the edge of his vision, something quick and flashy. He pointed towards it.

"That's a will-o'-the-wisp. Good. You've made a start."

"What's a will-o'... one of them?" asked Marcus.

"They're usually spirits who have fallen on hard times. Thieves from the Other Land use them to trick us. If you see one, look in the opposite direction. That's where the thing they are trying to hide will be."

"So, they're decoys?" asked Marcus. Tania nodded.

A roaring noise came from overhead, getting louder and louder. Marcus looked up, expecting to see the traffic helicopter. Instead, he saw an enormous dragon twenty metres up in the air, hovering over the pond. The water rippled with every wingbeat. A huge frog the size of a Labrador was hopping from lily pad to lily pad with a golden ball tucked under its front leg.

"That's what the will-o'-the-wisp was trying to distract you from." Tania shook her head, not at all disturbed by the deadly creature in the sky. "Feeble attempt."

"The dragon?"

"No, the frog thief. This is the last time it'll steal a dragon's egg, now that we're going to capture it!"

Then, to Marcus's surprise, Mrs Sunflower arrived on the scene. She charged towards the pond, knocking dog walkers and parked prams to one side. She didn't even stop for the water. She just carried on like a ship launched from a dock. The frog croaked and leapt. Mrs Sunflower reached out and grabbed it, dragging it into the shallow water. As they fell, she twisted so the frog ended up on top, hugged to her chest.

Quiz

Literal comprehension

Page 27 – What should you do if you see a will-o'-the-wisp?

Inferential comprehension

Pages 26–27 – What does Marcus see in this chapter that persuades him to believe everything that Tania has told him?

Prediction

What other crimes do you think Marcus might witness in the rest of the story?

Marcus was disappointed that he didn't get the apprenticeship at the film studio, but he soon discovered that his placement might be more exciting than he had imagined. He met Mrs Sunflower – a troll, and Tania – a firebird who took him on his first magical mission. At the park, he watched as a frog thief was captured after stealing a dragon's egg. What was going to be next?!

Reflection

What do you know about the Other Land and the people that come from there?

Prediction

Do you think that Marcus will be able to keep the details of his new job a secret from his friends and family?

Chapter 4

Marcus was impressed with what he had just seen.
"I see Mrs Sunflower is careful when making arrests,"
he said, surprised she had not squashed the frog or
the egg, even though she had charged straight in.

"She just doesn't want to scramble that egg,"
said Tania.

Dragging frog and egg back to the shore, Mrs
Sunflower squelched to the middle of the playground
to greet the dragon as it landed.

"How is nobody else seeing this?" Marcus asked. After
a few complaints about the gust of wind that knocked
them over, everyone in the park carried on as if
nothing was happening. "There's a
massive blue-and-silver dragon
on the playground."

"You'll work it out, soon enough," said Tania mysteriously.

The egg was returned to the dragon who tucked it into a pouch on its belly and took off. Mrs Sunflower tied up the frog and dragged it in the direction of the agency's headquarters. The frog kept croaking that it had done nothing wrong, but Mrs Sunflower wasn't interested.

"There you go," said Tania, "a classic takedown. Find, chase, arrest. Then return what was taken and leave the scene without any Normals seeing anything. That's what we want you to do."

Marcus gulped. "You want me to chase frog thieves?"

"Don't be silly. It won't always be frog thieves. You have to be ready to stop whatever trouble Otherworlders are causing. We want you to remember the steps," said Tania, patiently. "What are they?"

Marcus knew this. "Find, chase, arrest, return what was taken and make sure no one sees."

Tania nodded. "Exactly."

"So, what's my next mission?" asked Marcus.

"We want you to find proof that the werebats are threatening those who work for Mr Ali, our local baker."

* * *

Marcus was getting restless. When Tania had left him to stake out Mr Ali's patisserie, he thought he might get to go inside, pretend to be a customer or chat to the owner. But no. The rules were that he had to watch from across the road and keep out of sight until his substitute arrived.

The cake shop was well-lit with a window display of tempting treats. At least he could watch Gina Haskins learning to ice cupcakes. He had liked Gina since Year Seven but not yet got up the nerve to ask her on a date. Callum had said she was well out of his league. Marcus suspected Callum only said this because he had been shot down when he asked Gina to go to the prom last year. This had made Marcus feel like he had no chance. Still, it passed the time watching her pipe butter icing onto the trays of cakes, putting in little whirls and adding fondant butterflies and glitter.

There was no sign of any trouble in the shop as he trained his binoculars on the till. Mr Ali himself was an interesting man. When Marcus blinked and used his Other sight, the baker's legs were replaced by a misty, wispy haze and it appeared that he was actually floating above the ground, rather than standing.

"Marcus?"

He looked up to find a huge guy standing over him. At first, Marcus was terrified that he was about to be beaten up by a street tough. Then he realised that the boy knew his name.

"Yes?" Marcus replied, sounding uncertain.

"I'm Clive Sunflower. Half-troll in case you're wondering. I was the junior at my mum's business, until you arrived." He grinned, displaying two bottom teeth that curled up like tusks. "Pleased to meet you, short stuff."

"Good to meet you, er, big guy."

Clive crouched next to Marcus on the flat roof Tania had pointed out as the perfect lookout. The roof groaned under Clive's weight, but it didn't collapse.

"Got anything to eat?" asked Clive.

Marcus offered him the last of his stash from the dangerous cupboard.

"Thanks." Clive ate the bar, wrapper included, in one gulp. "I burn up fuel like a jet engine. Any developments?" He jerked his head to the shop opposite.

"Nothing so far. What is Mr Ali, by the way? Some kind of elf?"

"Nah, he's half-genie, which is good news for him because he won't get stuffed in a lamp and forced to grant wishes to greedy people. That can only happen to a full genie."

"What do you mean half-genie?" asked Marcus.

"All of us half-and-half folk have a human parent. Refugees from the Other Land usually settle down with someone from this world. Makes life easier and there are a lot more of them to fall in love with than Us refugees."

"So, if he's half-genie and got some of the powers, why can't Mr Ali wish his troubles away?"

"He could, but that would be a silly use of a wish," said Clive. "He gets three in his entire immortal life. Would you waste it on petty criminals making business difficult? No, you'd save it for a real emergency."

"People who get wishes from genies always make stupid choices," said Marcus as he rolled on to his back, letting Clive take over the watching. "Obviously, people should wish for world peace," Marcus continued.

"You can't. It would break even a full genie to attempt that. They might be able to manage a second of world peace, but then the world would go back to how it was and the wish would have been wasted. Same goes for ending hunger and everyone being happy."

"Mr Ali can only grant smaller wishes?" asked Marcus.

Marcus thought he would use his wish to become a famous director in a Hollywood studio.

"Tania warned me you had no clue about the rules. No, as a half-genie, he just gets three for *himself* in his lifetime. He can't grant them for other people. So don't go demanding stuff from him."

Marcus rolled back on his front. "I wouldn't!"

"It's cool, man, you're learning, but just remember all magic comes at a cost," said Clive. "You can't wave a wand and make stuff happen. That only happens in books. Real magic demands payment, so be very careful. There are other creatures that can grant wishes, but if you ask for something from the wrong person, you might find yourself becoming a servant to the Others or handing over your first-born child for them to raise."

"Wow, that's harsh," said Marcus. "Got it – no magical deals."

"Right, what's this?" Clive put the binoculars to his little, red eyes. "This might be one of the werebats."

Marcus blinked furiously, but the woman in a leather skirt and jacket remained exactly as she was. He was expecting to see batwings at the very least!

Quiz

Literal comprehension
Page 31 – What is a 'Normal'?

Inferential comprehension
Page 33 – What does the description of Mr Ali suggest about him?

Personal response
What would you wish for if you were a half-genie with three wishes to last your entire immortal life?

Chapter 5

These magical creatures were taking some getting used to. "I can't see anything special about her," said Marcus.

"You won't, not unless she shifts into a bat. Right now, she is in her human shape," explained Clive.

"How can you tell?" asked Marcus. "Will she hang upside down like a bat to make her order?"

"Yeah, you're so funny – not. After a while, you get to know what each group of shifters like. Werebats like bikes. They form motorbike gangs and zoom around in flocks. Leather is their go-to outfit."

"And how do you know they're a shifter to start with?" wondered Marcus.

Clive pointed at his face. "Something about the eyes. They always have a hint of their animal nature about them."

Marcus took the binoculars to check out the werebat. The woman had glittering dark eyes with a hint of a sneer. Gina was serving the woman, smiling and chatting as she did with all the customers. She was obviously good at her job, ignoring the woman's cold manner and remaining polite even as the customer stabbed a finger at the chocolate cakes she wanted. The biggest giveaway that something was wrong came from Mr Ali. He backed into a corner and rubbed his gold bracelet nervously.

"I'd say that's proof," said Marcus. "The werebat woman is making Mr Ali miserable just by being in the shop."

"If Mr Ali's word was enough, then the bats would've been run out of town long ago. Otherworlders like the bat shifters can only be punished if they threaten humans," explained Clive.

"So Mr Ali can be bullied by the werebats, but unless they threaten a human, there's nothing we can do about it? That seems wrong to me," said Marcus.

"Yeah, I agree, but the Other police won't help unless we find proof that the werebats have threatened not just Mr Ali but also his human wife and staff. As you can see, the werebat is being okay with the girl. She is rude, but she's not crossing any lines."

"That's Gina Haskins," said Marcus. "She goes to my school."

"Great! You can ask her if they've ever threatened her. If she makes a complaint, we've got them," said Clive. "Werebats are difficult creatures to catch in the act, but we might get them yet."

* * *

"So how was your first day?" Mum asked as she put her shopping bag on the kitchen counter. Marcus's little sister ran past him, heading straight for the TV. The rule was: the one who got the controller chose the programmes until bedtime. Marcus played along, not because he had any wish to watch TV, but because his little sister was his favourite person in the whole wide world.

She'd had a serious illness when she was a baby and they all thought they would lose her. She was so brave during her illness and that made her extra special for the whole family. He'd do anything for her, even if he would rather go and lie on his bed with the lights off to stop his head from spinning.

"Darn it, you beat me, you rotter!" he said, wrestling Mabel to the sofa and tickling her as she held the controller out of his reach.

"You get to pick your silly programmes."

"They're not silly!" declared Mabel.

"They so are!" He blew a raspberry on her arm.

"Urk!" She grinned as she wiped it off on her pink leggings. "Mummy, Marcus is being yucky again."

"Marcus?" called Mum from the kitchen area. "Come tell me about your first day."

Marcus went to help her unpack. "It was fine." Dragons, giant frogs, werebats and watching Gina ice cakes all afternoon were all the things that Marcus was thinking about – but of course, he said none of this to his mum.

"And what was the company?" asked his mum.

"Er..." He really needed a cover story, but he also didn't want to lie to his mother. "They find... um... people."

"Oh, so they find people to fill job vacancies? That's not so bad then. Who are you working with?"

"My boss is a lady called Tania – she reminds me a bit of a character from a Manga comic. Big eyes and bright red hair," Marcus described. "There's another boy called Clive. He's the son of the top boss, but he's okay. His mum is scary but I didn't spend much time with her."

His mum paused and looked at him. "That's a much longer answer to 'how was your day' than I usually get. I'm liking this apprenticeship scheme already."

Marcus grinned. "And how was your day?"

His mum patted her heart. "All this grown-up behaviour: it's too much! My day was fine." Marcus laughed. "Actually, it was great. Your dad rang. He finishes on the oil rig in a few days and will be home for two whole weeks," she continued.

Mabel whooped from the sofa. "Daddy is coming home!"

"That's good." But Dad might be a little more curious about what his son did at Sunflower and Co if he were at home on holiday rather than out at work all day like Mum. He'd have to make sure Dad didn't call in at the office. "Let me finish unpacking," he told mum. "Is your ankle better?"

"Thanks, love. It's getting there."

Marcus put the tins up in the cupboard. "Mum, er, have you ever noticed something odd if you blink hard?"

"Sorry?" She took a packet of fish fingers out of the freezer. "Are you having trouble with your eyes? Do you need an eye test? Glasses?"

"It's nothing. Just something that came up at work," answered Marcus.

"My boy at work." Mum smiled proudly. "Who knows? If you do well, maybe they'll ask you to stay on?"

When Marcus went in to wish his little sister goodnight and put her teddies in their line-up for the night, she patted the bed beside her. "Marcus?" Her big, brown eyes met his.

"Yes, Mabel-mine. What's up?"

"The sky? The sun?" He laughed and applauded. Mabel giggled. She loved it when Marcus liked her jokes. "Marcus, you know what you asked Mum, about blinking?"

He answered slowly. "Yes?"

"Sometimes, I see stuff, like fairytale stuff, but more scary. That's why I need the teddies in their places."

Marcus looked at the row of toys standing guard at the window. He had thought it was just a comforting routine Mabel had to help her sleep.

"The teddies will keep the bad things out, won't they?"
She sounded doubtful.

Marcus brushed a strand of hair off her cheek. "Mabel-
mine, not just the bears, but Mum, Dad and me. We'll
all make sure no bad things touch you." And the first
question he was going to ask at work tomorrow was
how to keep the Others out of his little sister's bedroom.
Somehow, he didn't think teddy bears would cut it.

Quiz

Literal comprehension
What do you learn about Marcus's sister,
Mabel, in this chapter?

Inferential comprehension
How would you describe Marcus's relationship
with his sister?

Prediction
What do you think will happen when Marcus's
dad comes back?

Chapter 6

On Wednesday, all the apprenticeship students were expected back at school to check in with the careers adviser. Marcus hung around Ms Faye's office, hoping to catch Gina. But first, he ran into Callum.

"Yo, bro, how's Sunflower?" Callum swaggered over. No need to ask how his apprenticeship was going.

Marcus bumped fists. "It's cool, man."

"What they got you doing?" asked Callum.

"We're headhunting, you know: finding people for jobs? Checking references – that stuff," lied Marcus.

Callum's eyes were already glazing over. "Okay, so it's not too bad?"

"It's fine," nodded Marcus.

Callum looked relieved. "That's great. I'm pleased for you. You had me worried for a moment."

Marcus knew he had to ask. "What's it like at Pinewood?"

Callum leaned in, dropping his voice as if he was sharing top-secret information. "On my first day, I was sorting out the paperwork for the *Star Wars* people. You wouldn't believe how many receipts for lunch they have."

"Filing?" asked Marcus.

"Yeah, and yesterday I got to sweep up the sawdust in the carpenters' workshop. They're making a set for Bond, some super-spy office, but it's all very hush-hush. I had to sign papers."

"I get you. My apprenticeship is a bit like that."

Marcus wished he could shout, "Callum, there are dragons!" and "the dreamcatchers they sell in shops really do work to protect bedrooms from nightmare creatures", but he knew he had to keep his mouth shut. He remembered what Tania had said about the code of conduct. He'd taken home a dreamcatcher yesterday and told Mabel it would do the trick, but that was as much as he could admit to anyone outside Sunflower.

A student came out of Ms Faye's office. "Next," called Ms Faye and Callum disappeared inside with a thumbs up.

Marcus was about to sit down on one of the chairs outside Ms Faye's office when Gina turned up. She was running to get to her appointment on time.

"Hey, Gina?" began Marcus.

"Sorry – late – been at work." She went straight in as Callum exited and closed the door behind her.

He was still waiting for his appointment when Gina came out of the office.

"Oh, hi again," she said awkwardly. He wanted to talk to her about the werebats. But what should he say?

"How is your apprenticeship going? I passed by the patisserie on the way to mine. It looks like a really great place to work," said Marcus before Gina had time to walk away.

Gina's face instantly lit up. "Oh, Marcus, it's just the best. I'm learning so much. Mr Ali is really patient and he's got this magic touch with pastries. I haven't seen anything quite as beautiful as his spun sugar and his éclairs are to die for."

"Then I'll have to stop by and try some," laughed Marcus.

"If you come when I'm on the till, I'll make sure you get the mate's rate," said Gina with a smile on her face.

He couldn't help beaming like a fool – she thought of him as a friend! He hadn't been sure she even knew his name. "Mate's rate?"

She wrinkled her brow. "I guess. I mean, I can give you the ones I spoil or aren't quite baked right. We're allowed to take those home. Where are you working?"

Marcus wanted to learn a bit more about the patisserie. He would really impress Clive if he could find out more about what was going on in the shop.

"Oh, I'm working for a headhunter company," explained Marcus. "They try to match people to jobs. They're nice. I was wondering, do you get any trouble in the shop, like thieves or people trying to get money out of you?"

She laughed and shook her head. "It's very hard to nick stuff as it's all behind glass for hygiene reasons.

And all the customers are lovely, just so pleased to be going home with a treat."

"*All* the customers are nice to you?"

"Nearly all." She looked confused, then glanced down as her phone chimed. "Have to dash. I'm expected back."

"But I thought today was a day we spent in school, not in our apprenticeship placements?" questioned Marcus.

"Mr Ali had to go see some people, so I said I'd help," explained Gina. "Ms Faye gave me permission. Might see you around, if you're working locally?"

"Count on it," smiled Marcus.

Marcus was wondering who Mr Ali could be meeting. Could it be something to do with the werebats? Gina looked a little surprised by his enthusiastic response.

"I'm reliably informed that the éclairs should be on my bucket list," said Marcus quickly.

She grinned and ran off. Forget Mr Ali's pastries, thought Marcus, she seemed even more magical.

Then Marcus heard Ms Faye's voice. "Marcus, I can see you now."

Marcus walked into Ms Faye's office. There was something about her that puzzled him. He would never have noticed it if he hadn't met Tania. Then Marcus decided to do something. He gave two slow blinks. Suddenly, he saw a kettle over a log fire and a black cat asleep on a rug. Blinking again, all he saw was the cat.

"Would you like something to drink?" asked Ms Faye. "Tea? Coffee?"

"Just water, please."

Marcus watched carefully as she filled a glass from the jug on her desk.

Marcus blinked, but the water remained water. Was he imagining things? Could Ms Faye possibly be an Usworlder? Tania and Clive had warned him about accepting food or drink from fairyland. Was he being too suspicious? He had known Ms Faye for years. Surely, she wasn't one of them?

"How is the placement going?" she asked.

"It's fine."

She put the water down in front of him. "Only fine?"

"I like it. It's challenging." He couldn't tell her about it without breaking the code of conduct. If she knew what was really going on, she would have to give him more clues. "Ms Faye," said Marcus. "How did Sunflower and Co get to be on our apprenticeship scheme?"

"The school has good connections with Sunflower and Co."

"So you've sent other apprentices to them?"

She gave a toss of her head and Marcus thought her long, dark braid moved rather oddly. He could've sworn it wriggled slightly.

"We only send special students to Sunflower and Co," she said.

Quiz

Literal comprehension
Page 50 – What does Marcus take home for his sister – and why?

Inferential comprehension
Pages 54–56 – Look again at the description of Marcus's meeting with Ms Faye. What do you learn about Ms Faye?

Personal response
What would you tell Ms Faye about your placement if you were Marcus?

The story so far

Marcus was sent on his first proper mission –
staking out Mr Ali's bakery, where Gina also
works. He met Mrs Sunflower's son, Clive, who
told Marcus more about some of the magical
creatures he'd met so far, including the
notorious werebats. Back at school, Marcus
speaks to the careers adviser, Ms Faye – who
tells him that only special students get sent to
do apprenticeships with Sunflower and Co...

Reflection

Why do you think that Marcus and Mabel are
both able to use their Other sight to see things,
but other characters can't?

Prediction

Do you think that Marcus will stop the
werebats from threatening
Mr Ali? How?

Chapter 7

Marcus was in Ms Faye's office talking to her about his apprenticeship. "Have Sunflower and Co told you what they do there?" asked Marcus.

"I'm afraid they didn't have much time to say anything to me. The last one, Martina Castrol, had an accident at work and didn't go back," explained Ms Faye.

"An accident?" Marcus squeaked.

"Fell off a wall, or down some steps, something like that," said Ms Faye. "Had her leg in plaster for six weeks. She decided not to return without danger money and the school couldn't afford that."

"And yet you thought it a good idea to send me there after that?"

"Oh yes. Martina's placement was long ago," said Ms Faye cheerily.

"How long?" asked Marcus suspiciously.

"I forget exactly, but certainly a long time ago. I'm sure you'll have a *magical* time there. Give my best to Mrs Sunflower and send Elena in."

Was using the word 'magical' like that a hint that Ms Faye knew what went on at Sunflower and Co? Confused, Marcus got up to send in the next student.

"Elena, how is the salon?" said Ms Faye briskly. "Do you still want to go into hairdressing?"

Marcus looked back and the black cat blinked at him, turning briefly into something much larger and scarier. Ms Faye knew all about the strange world of Sunflower and Co, he was almost sure of it.

Like Gina, Marcus also decided to spend the rest of the day at work rather than stay in school. Tania was out which meant he had to deliver his report to Clive.

"I found out that Mr Ali was out meeting people today, leaving the shop understaffed," Marcus told Clive.

"Useful information," said Clive, writing in the case file. "Tania is keeping an eye on Mr Ali today, so we should find out who he is meeting."

Marcus pointed at the screen on Clive's desk. "Why don't you use the computer?"

"That's not a computer," said Clive, shaking his head. "We don't have human technology here. It doesn't usually work for Usworlders, so Mum doesn't see the point."

"What are these screens then?" asked Marcus.

"Windows. Magic ones. What do you want to see?"

Clive tapped the screen. "It's got to be something you have a right to look at. If we are on a case, we get permission to monitor clients' homes; otherwise, it's public spaces."

"Like CCTV?" asked Marcus.

"Yeah, kinda. What's your pick?"

"Can I see my dad?" asked Marcus.

"If he's somewhere we're allowed to see." Clive wrote something on the screen with his fingertip.

The screen went from black to high definition. There was his dad going down a long ladder as waves slapped at the columns that supported the drilling platform of the oil rig. He was dressed in bright orange protective gear and a hard hat. Even though the sea was rough and the supply boat was rocking up and down, Marcus's dad had a big grin on his face. He really was coming home.

"Thought as much," said Clive as he shut off the screen.

"Thought what?" asked Marcus.

"You'll work it out. Not my place to tell you." Before Marcus could ask a follow-up question, Tania rushed in.

"We've got trouble! Mr Ali met with the bat colony today. The werebats have said they will burn down his bakery unless he pays them fifty gold pieces!"

"Is that a lot?" asked Marcus. Tania and Clive looked at him in amazement.

"It's only like five million human pounds!" said Tania. "Yes, I'd say that's a lot."

"How is a baker supposed to get hold of that much money?" asked Marcus.

"A *half-genie* baker." Tania stroked Beckham, who appeared not to have moved from the filing cabinet all week.

"By wishing for it, of course. They want him to use one of his three wishes. But if he gives in, then any Other gang could turn the screws, forcing Mr Ali to waste all his wishes paying them off. When the fourth gang comes, his bakery burns down and he's left with nothing."

"Can't he wish the bad guys away?" asked Marcus.

"Do you remember why you couldn't use a magic wish to wish for world peace? You can manage it for a short while, but they'll keep coming back like flies on dung," said Clive glumly. "I don't suppose they did us a favour and threatened your friend?"

"Gina says all the customers are okay with her," said Marcus. "I guess the Otherworlders know not to break the law. You should really change the rules and make it illegal for them to threaten you."

"Threaten *us*," corrected Clive. "You're one of us now."

"So, just like you, I can be threatened without being able to do anything about it. That sounds great," said Marcus.

"He's getting sarcastic with us. Must mean he's settling in," Tania said to Clive.

"What do you think Mr Ali will do?" asked Marcus.

"He's talking about moving his business out of London," said Tania.

"But if he does that, the bullies win!" Marcus was also thinking that if Mr Ali moved out of London, Gina would lose her dream job.

"But at least the werebats don't get to steal one of Mr Ali's wishes," said Tania. "It's not great, but it might be the best we can hope for. Now, I've got to get back on duty. Clive, be sure to tell your mum what I saw."

Clive saluted her. "Will do. Stay safe out there," he said.

"If there's trouble, I'm very difficult to catch," laughed Tania. She flew up the hole left for the pole, showing exactly why she was very difficult to catch.

On his way home, Marcus wondered what he could do to help. He had to capture the moment when a werebat said something bad to Gina or Mr Ali. It would be easy to monitor this happening if he could break into the patisserie once it had closed, rig up one of his cameras and set it recording inside the bakery.

He could monitor the feed on his computer. But how to make the werebats angry enough to forget their caution and have a go at the human staff? That was the challenge.

The werebats were regular customers, arriving near closing time each day. Marcus searched on his phone for what scares off bats and dismissed most of the suggestions as impossible.

But one suggestion caught his eye. Bats hate cinnamon. Perfect. All he had to do was make sure the patisserie gave the werebats treats topped with cinnamon, sit back and wait for the fireworks. Marcus was very pleased with his plan.

Quiz

Literal comprehension
Page 62 – What does Tania discover about Mr Ali and the werebats in this chapter?

Inferential comprehension
Page 62 – Clive shows Marcus his dad through the 'magic window'. Clive says, ' Thought as much... Not my place to tell you.' What do you think this means?

Prediction
Do you think Marcus's plan will work? Why? Why not?

Chapter 8

Marcus began to have doubts as to the wisdom of breaking into the patisserie after hours when he caught sight of a blue cat watching him.

"Psst! Beckham! Shoo!"

The cat ignored him. It lifted a paw and began to wash. Marcus climbed onto the wheelie bin behind the shop and slid into an open window. No money was kept in the till overnight, so the security wasn't tight. He wriggled through the small window and into the staff bathroom. From there, he could access the shop. Marcus had already picked the spot where he would hide his camera. Behind the till, there was a display of the different kinds of loaves you could buy. He rigged his camera to a baguette, lens pointing directly at where the customer stood. He attached the microphone to a round loaf.

His heart almost leapt out of his chest when something clattered to the ground in the back room. Beckham strolled into the bakery.

"You almost gave me a heart attack!" gasped Marcus.

The cat blinked at him.

"I'm not stealing anything. I'm trying to help."

Beckham twitched his tail.

"No, it's a good plan. Trust me."

The cat stalked out.

"You'll see."

* * *

The next day, Marcus left his lookout post on the roof over the road from the patisserie just before the werebat woman was expected.

He strolled into the shop to find Gina on the till. That was lucky.

"Hey, Marcus, lovely to see you."

"And you. I said I'd drop by."

"You did. Now what can I get you? We've some wonky lemon cupcakes I can let you have."

That wouldn't do at all. "Can I have four cinnamon rolls, two of your cinnamon and vanilla slices, and six cinnamon doughnuts," asked Marcus.

"Like a bit of cinnamon, do you?" asked Gina grinning as she bagged up his picks. The total was most of the money in his pocket, but he hoped this would be the best twenty pounds he'd ever spent. The bag had to be big enough.

"Have you finished work already?" Gina asked as she handed over his change.

"I can finish when I want. It's very flexible."

"I finish at 5.30 if you are still around," said Gina.

Marcus almost missed what Gina said as he could hear a motorbike approaching. "Oh, I can be here. Walk you home?"

"That'd be nice," smiled Gina, shyly.

Just then, the werebat woman came in.

"My usual order." Her voice was high, like the noise of a dentist's drill.

"Of course. I'll just get it ready." Gina began loading up a bag with a selection of cakes, heavy on the chocolate and cream. She placed it on the counter and announced the total.

"Hey, is that parking warden about to ticket that bike outside?" said Marcus.

"What!" screeched the woman, rushing to the door. Even Gina moved to the window to look. Marcus quickly swapped the bags.

"I can't see anyone," said Gina. "Are you sure?"

"Must've turned down the other street," said Marcus. "See you later, Gina." He hurried out before either of them noticed that he was carrying a bag loaded with chocolate cake and éclairs.

Back on the roof, he munched on an éclair while he watched the shop. Gina was beginning the closing time routine, washing the cabinets and putting unsold items into the fridge. Mr Ali checked on her occasionally but went back to finishing the wedding cake he was carefully decorating.

Marcus was beginning to fear that the werebats hadn't noticed their treats had been swapped, or maybe they were perfectly happy with cinnamon?

Then three motorbikes zipped up the high street and parked outside the shop. The riders got off as if they were all moving as one.

That's the bat behaviour showing through, thought Marcus. He began to worry that he'd put Gina in danger. The two women and one man stormed into the shop. They didn't look friendly. Gina's smile dimmed. Marcus couldn't hear what was said, but from the waving arms and thumps on the counter, it wasn't pretty. Gina looked over her shoulder to the back room, evidently hoping to be rescued. Mr Ali rushed in and stood in front of Gina. From the angry movements, Marcus feared it was getting too heated. He'd have to go over there and intervene. But how exactly? Bring back the bag and claim it was his fault?

Then Mr Ali opened the till and grabbed a handful of notes. He shoved them at the woman.

The biker glanced at them, stuffed them in her pocket and signalled to her friends to leave. As a final act of meanness, she shoved Mr Ali with her were-strength through the door into the back room. He hit the table and, of course, the wedding cake wobbled and toppled over, landing in a crash of icing and fruit cake.

Marcus gasped. Look what he'd done! He had to hope the footage on his hidden camera made up for the chaos he had caused. This had been a terrible plan.

* * *

Marcus arrived home feeling awful. Gina had been really upset on their walk home. A customer had pushed Mr Ali, she'd told him, all because she was angry with Gina. She couldn't understand how the mix-up with the order had happened. She had asked Marcus if he'd noticed he'd picked up the wrong order and he lied, saying he'd just dropped it off at work and not checked.

"I don't know how it happened," Gina had said. "Maybe I'm not cut out for this kind of work? I hate it when customers shout at me."

This was the exact opposite of what Marcus wanted to achieve. He wanted to save her job, not make her doubt herself.

Once he was alone in his bedroom, Marcus downloaded the footage. "This had better be good," he muttered.

And it was. The werebat woman strutted around the little screen, yelling insults and demanded her money back.

"As for you, you silly human girl, I'll see you never work in this city again!" she shouted at one point. "Poison my flock, would you?"

That was the money shot. He clipped out that section and captioned it 'Epic Overreaction'.

Gina needed to see it wasn't her but the customer who was at fault. He shared it with her saying,

"Found this online. That customer totally lost it. You are not to blame." He pressed send. Then he sent the same clip to Clive – he was the only one at Sunflower and Co who had a phone. This one he tagged 'Proof'.

Chapter 9

Marcus arrived at work expecting to be asked to perform a lap of honour. He had totally rocked, solving his first mission all on his own. So it was surprising to find glum faces when he arrived at the warehouse. Even Beckham had hidden behind his tail.

"Hey, guys, what's up?" he asked.

"Mrs Sunflower wants to see you," said Tania. Clive just shook his head. Marcus knocked on Mrs Sunflower's door.

"Come!"

Was this how prisoners felt when hearing their sentence?

"Mrs Sunflower." He stood and she made no gesture towards the chair.

"Do you understand what you've done?" she asked.

"Er, got you the proof you needed to shut down the werebat gang threats?"

"And how did you do that?"

"I filmed them." He wondered if he was in trouble for using human technology to film the werebats. "I'm sorry, I got my camera back. No one will know how we did it – and I won't do it again."

"No one will know?" She held up Clive's phone. "Look."

With horror, he saw his little clip had been posted on a video sharing site, but with music and filters, so the woman now had bat ears and fangs. And views? Ten thousand and rising.

"Clive posted the video of the werebats?"
Marcus asked.

"Clive? Of course not, you... you..." Mrs Sunflower's eyes glowed like hot coals, and steam came from her snout. She took a deep breath, trying to control her anger. "No. Did you send it to anyone else?"

"The girl who works at the shop." In a blinding flash, Marcus realised what must have happened. Gina had posted the video online.

"And *she* decided to have a little revenge on the werebat who had ruined her day," shouted Mrs Sunflower. "To cheer herself up, she posted it on a thread for impossible customers and added the bells and whistles you see. She obviously chose bat ears and fangs as the filter, just to make the woman look foolish."

"I think—" began Marcus.

"No, you *don't* think, Marcus. You've destroyed centuries of secrecy about our existence in one tap of a button. You've broken the first rule of our code."

Tania knocked on the door. "What?" snarled
Mrs Sunflower.

"Before you murder him, I will say in his defence that
he isn't the first to expose our existence."

Mrs Sunflower growled. "Don't remind me."

"Will Shakespeare even used my full name, Titania,
and made a play about us."

"It never, ever goes away," said Mrs Sunflower. "I'm
through with apprentices. Marcus is our last mistake
in that department!"

"But I also came in to say Morgan has heard about the
trouble and she's coming here," said Tania.

Mrs Sunflower gulped. "Morgan?"

"Afraid so. Prepare for an inspection by the Chief of
Other Police."

* * *

Marcus felt it was like sitting on the naughty step when he was given the duty of clearing out Beckham's litter tray. The task was grim, but better than being with his colleagues who were rapidly completing their paperwork and preparing their reports. Whoever this Morgan was, she made even a troll quake in her boots.

The door crashed open and a lady in a green robe stood in the entrance, black cat at her side. Beckham hissed and arched his back.

"Chief Inspector," said Mrs Sunflower, at the same time as Marcus said "Ms Faye!"

The careers adviser glanced at him. "Morgan La Faye is my full name, and no, I won't be answering your questions. We have an emergency."

"You saw the video?" asked Marcus.

"How could I miss it?" she snapped. "Every student at school is watching it because they all know Gina."

"And the werebats?"

"They are demanding the one who exposed them be dealt with to the full extent of the law."

"Meaning?" asked Tania fearfully.

"Execution by their flock."

"You can't hurt Gina!" Marcus blurted out. "It's not her fault!"

"No, indeed, she is a human, so the law doesn't apply to her," said Ms Faye. "And I agree that she isn't to blame."

"And I'm human too," Marcus sighed with relief.

Ms Faye shook her head. "You are only half right. Unfortunately, half of you has its origin in the Other Land, which brings you under the scope of our law."

"What? No! I'm human. Ask Mum and Dad," pleaded Marcus.

"You ask them. I think you'll be surprised by the answer." Ms Faye swept her cloak aside and sat in the chair that Clive carried to her. "So, what are we to do? Marcus, you caused this problem. Do you have any ideas?"

Marcus was still reeling from all the revelations. "But you're a careers adviser. How can you also be the Chief of Other Police?"

"Yes," explained Ms Faye. "As Chief of Other Police, I deal with Usworlder refugees. Schools are a great place for me to find young half-humans. I had you on my list from your first day. Waiting six years for you to mature is nothing for an immortal." She turned to Mrs Sunflower. "I don't want to lose another apprentice."

"Yes, that incident with the ogre was very unfortunate," Mrs Sunflower agreed.

"Martina was never the same after that. Except for this video, how has Marcus been doing?" asked Ms Faye.

"A little slow to pick things up but not totally hopeless," said Mrs Sunflower.

Tania sneaked up behind him and whispered, "That's high praise from Mrs S."

"So worth saving?" asked Ms Faye.

"I'd say so," Mrs Sunflower scowled.

"Let's see if he can save himself then." Ms Faye turned to him. "Marcus, what's your plan?"

"My plan?" said Marcus.

"Yes." Ms Faye watched him with the same cool gaze as her cat.

"Yes, I totally have a plan," said Marcus, thinking quickly. "A clever one. A really, really amazing idea."

"He doesn't have a plan," said Tania with a sigh. "It's been nice knowing you."

"Wait! Give me a chance," begged Marcus.

Ms Faye stood up. "You have twenty-four hours to make this go away, Marcus, or I'll have to give you to the werebat flock and let them deal with you. Understood?" She swept out, her cat making a final swipe at Beckham, who dodged behind Clive.

Silence fell. Marcus could feel all eyes on him.

"An apprenticeship isn't school; this is real life with real-life consequences," said Mrs Sunflower.

"We'll help him, right?" said Tania, looking at her colleagues.

"Yeah," said Clive, "but he's doomed. What can we do?"

"I could fly him out of here – take him to my nest in the mountains for a few months," suggested Tania.

"I don't think the bats would let you get away with that. They won't forget," said Clive.

Chapter 10

Marcus folded his arms across his chest, feeling hollow inside. "Will the werebats really kill me?"

Tania's eyes flickered to Clive. "Well..."

"Yeah, they will, bro," said Clive.

"Have I really exposed them?" asked Marcus. "Can't we claim it was all just play-acting, like you did with William Shakespeare?"

Tania shook her head. "You don't get it, do you? They think you told your girlfriend about them and that was why she chose the bat filter."

"But I didn't!" said Marcus desperately.

"But how to prove it?" Tania fluttered in a circle. "Of all the filters in all the world, she chose that one. It doesn't feel random."

"That woman started it with her screeching about poisoning her flock!" said Marcus.

"We can still prove they issued threats to a human, so Mr Ali is safe, but that doesn't save you," said Mrs Sunflower.

"I'll think of something," said Marcus.

Mrs Sunflower gave him a pitying look. "Go home and spend what time you have left with your family. Your dad should be back this afternoon, shouldn't he?"

"How do you know...?" He looked at the magic window. "Oh."

"They show us what Others are doing," said Mrs Sunflower. "He's almost home."

* * *

There was no one in when Marcus arrived in his flat. Mum was at work, Mabel was at nursery and Dad was still travelling. He put aside the hint that connected Dad with the Others. Had Dad become an Usworlder refugee, or did he go away so often because he still lived in the Other London? Marcus could ask him about that if he survived. Right now, he needed every brain cell to come up with a plan. But his mind was blank.

His gaze fell on his *Star Wars* film poster. Would he ever see Callum again? It seemed petty to have envied Callum his job at Pinewood when really he should've been happy for his friend. Callum might have come late to movie-making, but Marcus didn't own the career.

Callum. Pinewood. Hanging out with actors... suddenly, Marcus's brain was back in gear. He sprang up and called his friend.

The next morning, Marcus answered the summons to Ms Faye's office. He decided not to involve his colleagues at Sunflower and Co. If his idea had failed, then he shouldn't drag them into the trouble he had caused. And he was already worried that he had got Gina into trouble at her apprenticeship too. Had he also ruined his chances of getting together with her?

"Come!" said Ms Faye.

When he entered this time, there was no disguise on the room. A black panther lay on the hearth rug and Ms Faye sat in a throne by a roaring log fire. Marcus blinked and briefly, it went back to the beige office he was used to seeing.

"Marcus, have you come up with a plan?" asked Ms Faye with more gentleness in her tone than he expected. She clearly thought she would be delivering him to a flock of bloodthirsty bats very shortly.

There was a brief tap on the door and the werebat woman walked in. *Oh no!* thought Marcus. His time was up. He was going to be handed over to the werebats right now. Sweat beaded on his brow.

"Jocinda, you're early." Ms Faye didn't sound pleased.

"Is this the boy? We'll take him from here," said the werebat.

"Er, I'd really rather you wouldn't," said Marcus hurriedly. "I've made the problem go away – or at least watered it down, like you did with Shakespeare."

Jocinda wasn't listening. She was already reaching for him.

"Hold!" barked Ms Faye. Jocinda froze.

"Very well," snapped Jocinda. "You have two minutes. Show me!"

Knowing his life was on the line, Marcus turned his phone screen around. "See here." He started playing a video called 'Batty customer #2'. A man with his face covered by the bat filter demanded crazy food stuffs from an anxious woman at a canteen.

"I don't see your point," said Ms Faye.

Marcus played 'Batty Customer #3', then #4.

"There are thirty-six of them, all out on the internet, all getting more views than the one in the bakery. There's even one with an actor from the next *Star Wars* movie. That one's gone viral," explained Marcus.

"How...?" asked Ms Faye.

"My friend is working at Pinewood and some of the actors had a lot of time on their hands. I asked him to film some improvised scenes for me saying it was for a training video my personnel company was putting together. How to handle difficult customers.

He thinks I'm just getting a gold star, not that he's saving my life."

Ms Faye looked at the video listings, then looked at Jocinda. "It looks to me like he has successfully crowded the field, so no one will investigate further. You are just one batty customer among many."

"And the hashtag is gaining new videos all over the world," added Marcus. "There are thirty-six now, but by tomorrow, there will be hundreds."

"I still want to kill him," hissed the werebat.

"Understandable, but no longer legal," said Ms Faye. "He's learned his lesson. I hope you've learned yours about not threatening humans? You'll be able to explain your side of that little argument at the next Other court. And I can already issue an order that you don't set foot in Mr Ali's bakery. There's a curse on you if you do."

"But my éclairs!" the werebat protested.

"Are they really worth dying for?" asked Ms Faye.

Jocinda scowled and hissed. Before Marcus's eyes, she began to shift, arms twisting, legs thinning. It looked painful. Finally, a vampire bat as big as a kite flapped out of a nest of leather clothes and flew out of the window.

"That was... cool," said Marcus.

"*Have* you learned your lesson, Marcus?" asked Ms Faye. "There is a rule that we extend to apprentices, that we forgive them three minor infringements of the code. You've lost one already. Do you want to go back? I can find you another assignment at the supermarket if you think it's too dangerous. You can put that side of your inheritance behind you."

Marcus met her cool green eyes. "No, I'm good. I'll see this through, thanks."

* * *

Dad was waiting for him by the school gate, his brown hair sleeked back from his forehead, his big, dark eyes shining with love and concern.

"Everything okay? What did she want with you?"

Marcus paused by the bike racks. "Do you know about Ms Faye?" Dad looked away over Marcus's head.

"Dad, what are you?"

His father grinned and threw his arm around Marcus's shoulders. "Now, wouldn't you like to know!"

"Yes, I would!"